No Problem

Dayle Campbell Gaetz

orca soundings

ORCA BOOK PUBLISHERS

National Library of Canada Cataloguing in Publication Data
Gaetz, Dayle, 1947-

No problem / Dayle Campbell Gaetz.

(Orca soundings)

ISBN 1-55143-231-5

I. Title. II. Series.

PS8563.A25317N62 2003   jC813'.54   C2002-911493-4

PZ7.G1185No 2003

First published in the United States, 2003

Library of Congress Control Number: 2002116520

Summary: Curt has it all: friends, summer job, a promising career in
baseball; then he begins experimenting with drugs.

Orca Book Publishers gratefully acknowledges the support for its
publishing programs provided by the following agencies: the
Government of Canada through the Book Publishing Industry
Development Program (BPIDP), the Canada Council for the Arts and
the British Columbia Arts Council.

Cover design: Christine Toller
Cover photography: Eyewire
Printed and bound in Canada

IN CANADA:
Orca Book Publishers
1030 North Park Street
Victoria, BC Canada
V8T 1C6

IN THE UNITED STATES:
Orca Book Publishers
PO Box 468
Custer, WA USA
98240-0468

07 06 05 04 • 5 4 3 2

For Bruce.
We miss you.
DCG

Chapter One

My first day on the job and Stuart was supposed to show me what to do.

"Open those boxes and put all the jars of pickles up there," he said. He pointed to a high shelf and a stepladder. Then he took off. That was it. Big lesson. I climbed the ladder and set to work.

Two minutes later I heard this husky voice, "So, are you the new kid?"

Dumb question. I looked down. The first

thing I saw was the top of a head with hair so blond it looked white. Except for this dark patch right on top. Two shiny blue eyes laughed up at me.

"Yup," I said, "that's me. The new kid."

"Come on down and meet Rachel."

"Sure. Okay." I climbed down the ladder and glanced around. "So, where's Rachel?"

She laughed, deep in her chest. Rachel was as tall as I was, but she was really thin. Her white-blond hair was cut short and straight, with bangs down to her dark eyebrows. She wore tons of makeup, which looked sort of sexy. Her full lips were as red as my baseball cap.

"So, the new kid's a comedian," she said. "What's your name, funny boy?"

"Curt."

A cool hand reached out to shake mine. "I'm Rachel," she said.

I gulped and backed up the ladder.

Rachel laughed again. "Nice meeting you, Curt." I watched her slink away.

Stuart and I took our lunch break together. We went through the stockroom and out the back door to take a shortcut across the mall.

"Hi, boys!"

We swung around. Rachel was sitting on a wooden bench. She crossed her long legs and took a drag on her cigarette.

"Hey, Rachel!" Stuart called. I waved and we walked away.

"What's with her?" I asked.

"She likes teasing the young guys," Stuart said. "But don't start thinking she'll go out with you or anything. It ain't gonna happen. Besides, she's way old!" He glanced at me. "Hey, man, did you hurt your pitching arm lifting those heavy cases?"

I realized I was rubbing my right shoulder. I dropped my hand. "They didn't feel heavy to me. Did you hurt yourself?"

Stuart flexed. "Me? Of course not. I'm way stronger than you! You're the one who keeps hurting your arm."

"It's fine." I didn't want to talk about it. My shoulder ached, but not too bad. I could handle it. I had no choice. Baseball season was about to start.

Dad was waiting on the back porch when I got home after work. He threw a baseball up and caught it. "So, Curt," he said, tossing me my glove. "How was your first day at work?"

"Okay."

"Come on." He stood up, grabbed his glove and headed for the backyard. "Let's see how that pitching arm is doing. This is going to be a big year for you."

We worked on my curveball until Mom called us in for dinner.

The next day at tryouts, Stuart and I both made the Falcons, the junior men's team. We were done with midget baseball, and the Falcons' coach was the best in the league. I knew Stuart would be awesome on first base. Coach Watson said I was the best pitcher he had seen in years.

That should keep my father happy. The thing is, back in the old days, he almost got to pitch for a major league team. Then he broke his arm and that was that. Now it's my turn.

Anyway, between baseball, school and my part-time job I didn't have time for much else. Until I met Leah.

I was kneeling on the floor, stocking cookie shelves, when this girl came flying around the corner. Her long legs and short shorts were the first things I saw. My mouth dropped open. I stood up, clutching a box of chocolate cookies. She smiled and I was lost. I think it was those dimples that got to me.

The day was hot and she wore a shimmery blue halter top. Her soft brown hair tumbled around her beautiful face and fell over her shoulders. Her huge eyes were dark like black coffee and full of sparkling lights. She had the cutest freckles across her cheeks and nose. Her breasts were perfect too. I stared at the blue cloth…and tore my eyes away.

"Thank you," she said.

My face went red. Did I say something? Did she know what I was thinking? "For what?" I squeaked.

She took the box from me. "How did you know I was looking for this kind of cookie?"

I grinned. "It's my job. We aim to meet our customers' every need."

"You're very good at your job." She turned and hurried off.

I stood still, gaping. Then I shook my head and followed. She wasn't in the next aisle, or the one after that. I spotted her in produce, pushing a shopping cart. I started towards her, but just then a tall, good-looking guy placed a big basket of strawberries in her cart.

"Mmm, those look good," she said. "Let's get some whipping cream and make a strawberry shortcake tonight."

I stopped to pick up a peach that had fallen to the floor, then walked on by, trying not to look at her.

It didn't work. My eyes rolled towards her. She winked. I grinned.

A week later I was standing on a ladder, putting packages of tea bags on the top shelf. That's where the manager wanted them. I'm guessing he liked to watch little old ladies jump up and down trying to reach the tea. I was up there, leaning towards the shelf, when I heard a voice. "Hey!"

My arms were loaded down with packages and I couldn't see a thing. I figured it must be Rachel. "Hey yourself!" I called.

"Got any more of those chocolate cookies?"

The top package started to slip. I made a grab for it, but the whole stack came apart in the middle. Every damn one of those packages flew out of my arms like they had sprouted wings. I lost my balance and started to tip sideways.

"Careful." A warm hand touched my elbow and helped to steady me. A thrill shot through me, like a jolt of electricity.

I swallowed, fixed a cool smile in place and looked down. *Whoa!*

I grinned like a total idiot.

Chapter Two

She was more gorgeous than I remembered. I climbed down the ladder and looked around for her boyfriend.

"The cookies are in Aisle 1. Same place as last week." I bent to pick up the packages of tea scattered all over the floor. If someone tripped on them, I would be in big trouble.

She crouched beside me. "I'll help you. It was my fault you dropped them."

When the tea was all picked up, she held half

of the packages while I climbed back up the ladder. She passed them to me until they were all neatly stacked, safely out of reach of your average tea drinker.

"So, do you get a coffee break or something?" she asked.

"Sure."

She waited.

"Want me to get those cookies for you?" I asked.

"No! I'll get them myself!" She turned and stomped away, pushing an empty shopping cart.

"Where's your boyfriend?" I called.

She stopped. "What boyfriend?"

"You know, the guy you were with last time I saw you?"

"You mean Darren? Tall, dark and so good-looking no girl can keep her hands off him?"

"Whatever." I didn't like where this was going.

"Darren's my brother. And in case you care, I'm Leah."

Half an hour later, on my break, we met at a little coffee shop in the mall.

"What school do you go to?" I asked.

9

"I don't. I'm finishing tenth grade by correspondence, but I'll go to Esquimalt Secondary in September. We just moved here and I'm not ready to start a new school."

"I go to Esquimalt too. I'm almost finished grade eleven."

"Awesome! At least I'll know someone. I'm kind of scared of the first day, you know?"

I nodded. "So, why did you move to Victoria? Did your parents get jobs here or something?"

She looked away. "Not exactly. My dad doesn't have a job right now. And my mom took off ages ago."

I changed the subject. "Do you always go shopping with your brother? I mean, how many guys take their sisters shopping?"

"My dad asked Darren to drive me that first day. Darren's doing okay. He moved to Victoria last year and got a job. He has his own apartment and a car."

I wracked my brain for a brilliant response. Anything to impress her. "Uh," I said.

She frowned. "So, what do you do besides work at the grocery store and go to school?" she asked.

"I dunno. Play baseball, swim and hang out

at the beach. What do you do?"

"Not much. I used to play baseball though, back home. And I like swimming. Maybe I'll look for a summer job."

"Speaking of jobs, I better go." I looked at Leah. "Hey, I've got a game on Saturday. Want to come and watch?"

She smiled. "Sure, okay. Sounds like fun."

"Great then, give me your phone number and I'll call you."

Leah came to the next three games. She must have brought me luck because I had never pitched better. We won those games without even trying. It helped me almost forget about my dad standing by the dugout. He had his arms folded across his belly and a scowl on his face like he had major gas pains. He always watched for every little mistake so he could tell me about it later. This usually made me nervous, but with Leah there I didn't even glance his way.

"Good game, Curt," Coach Watson said after the third game. "With you pitching, the Falcons can't lose!" Then he noticed me rubbing my shoulder. "Your arm hurting?"

"Not bad."

"I want you to lay off those curveballs for a while. They can damage your shoulder and elbow."

"I'm fine." A little ice, a little rest, and my arm would be good.

"Listen, Curt, a good friend of mine is a trainer for a major league team. He gave me these pills. They might help your shoulder." He pulled a small plastic bottle from his pocket.

I shook my head. "I'm fine," I said again.

"Hey, it's just a muscle relaxant." He patted my shoulder, "No sense in hurting when you don't need to. Look, just take this bottle so you'll have them in case you need one."

I tucked the bottle inside my baseball glove and started towards the stands.

"Their pitchers suck compared to you." Stuart caught up to me and slapped me on the back. "Hey, want to come over and watch a video?"

I looked towards the stands. Leah waved.

"Oh," Stuart grinned, "I guess not."

"See you at school, Stu," I said. I walked over to meet Leah.

"Good game," she said, standing on tiptoe to kiss me.

Whoa! Leah has the warmest, softest lips. I could wrap her in my arms and kiss her forever.

"Curt?"

"Huh?"

"I asked if you want to walk me home?"

"Sure, okay." I took her hand. "We could get something to eat too."

"I can't take long. I need to get home."

"What are you, Cinderella?"

"What?" She dropped my hand.

"I don't know, Leah. You're always in such a big rush to get home. How come?"

"That's my business!" she snapped. She forced a smile. "Curt, that's just the way it is. I can't stay out late. Besides, don't you have a math final in two days? You said you needed to study."

"Whatever."

"I think I'll walk home by myself," she said.

I couldn't let her go like this, both of us angry. "Come on, you have to eat. Let's go grab a burger."

She looked at me. Then she nodded and we walked in silence for a few blocks. She slipped her hand into mine. "I'm sorry," she said.

"Me too."

Chapter Three

When I opened the back door, my parents were sitting in the kitchen, eating pasta. They did not look happy.

"Where have you been?" Mom asked. "We expected you home for dinner. I saved some for you."

I shook my head. "That's okay, Mom. I had a burger with Leah."

Her lips pulled into a straight line. "Do you think you could let me know next time?"

"Sure, Mom, okay."

Dad drummed his fingers on the table. "As you may have noticed, I was at the game," he said. "You took off before we could talk."

"Oh, yeah, sorry."

"You pitched a good game, son."

That caught me by surprise. "Thanks, Dad."

"I bet you can hardly wait for the big league scouts to come calling."

"Yeah, sure, Dad." I reached up to rub my sore shoulder. "I think I'll take a shower." I left the room.

"Don't forget to study for math!" my mother called.

In my room, I tossed my baseball glove at the desk. Something fell out and rolled across the floor. The pill bottle. I picked it up and took it into the bathroom. I took one pill and stood in the shower, letting the hot water massage my shoulder. When I climbed into bed, I fell asleep in two seconds.

By the morning my arm felt great.

I felt good all day at school. I felt terrific when I went to work.

Rachel was in the stockroom. She flicked her

blond hair away from her face and winked at me. "Hiya, handsome. Want to share the good news?"

I grinned. "I just feel good today."

"I'm happy for you," she said softly. She moved closer and her blue eyes gazed into mine. "How about we go out after work and celebrate?"

"Uh…" Rachel and me? She's got to be at least twenty-three or twenty-four. She was watching me, a little smile on her lips.

"Uh…" I said again. "Sorry, I have to study math."

She raised one eyebrow. "Too bad," she said.

After work I really did think about going home to study. For about two seconds. Then I walked over to Leah's apartment.

"Hi, it's me," I said when she answered the intercom.

"Curt?" a mechanical voice crackled through the speaker.

"Yeah."

"I'll be right down."

I waited. She never invited me in. I wondered why. Maybe she didn't want her dad to know about me. Maybe she was embarrassed. I was going to ask her about it, but when she walked out the door and smiled at me, I forgot about it.

We watched a movie. At least, we sat in the back of the theater while a movie played. I have no idea what it was. Then we got something to eat and walked back to her place with our arms around each other.

Outside her building she took my hand and led me behind a big spruce tree away from the lights. She wrapped her arms around my neck and pressed her body close to mine.

We kissed. Her lips were so warm and she felt so good in my arms, I wanted to take her home with me. I slipped my hands under her shirt; her skin was like soft silk.

"I've got to go now," she said and pushed me gently away. We walked back to the door.

"Good-night, Curt," she said.

"Good-night." I kissed her again. "See you at the game tomorrow?"

"Wouldn't miss it."

Dad was watching TV when I got home. I crashed on the couch.

"About time you got here," he snapped. "Where have you been?"

"I had a date with Leah."

"I thought you'd come home. We always practice the night before a game."

I felt bad. I didn't mean to disappoint him. "Sorry."

"You should be!" he growled. "You don't practice, you stay out late chasing after some girl…"

"Her name's Leah and I wasn't chasing after her!"

"You'll let the Falcons down tomorrow!"

"Dad, it's just a game…"

"Not for you! You'll never make the big leagues if you don't work at it. What's wrong with you?"

"Nothing," I said. I almost told him then. I almost said, *I don't want to be a professional baseball player!* I didn't know how to tell him.

The thing is, ever since I was a little kid, my dad bragged to everyone that one day I would be some famous baseball star. And I have to admit I wasn't bad. Not good enough for the big leagues, but not bad. I just wished he would ask me what I wanted.

"What's all this shouting about?" Mom came into the room.

"No one's shouting," Dad told her. "I was

only reminding Curt that he needs to work hard if he's going to be the best."

"The best what?"

"Pitcher!" he shouted. "He's got a real shot at it."

"The important thing is that Curt enjoys the game." She turned to me. "Did you and Leah have a good time tonight?"

Before I could answer, my father interrupted. "Don't you get it, Sarah? He shouldn't be out half the night before an important game!"

Mom ignored him. "Are you ready for your math test tomorrow?"

"Sure, Mom."

"That's good. I know you'll do well. You can't afford to get a bad mark."

This was supposed to make me feel better?

I got up from the couch. "I'm going to bed," I said.

Chapter Four

I sat at my desk and tried to concentrate. The numbers on the page swam in front of my eyes. None of it made any sense. School used to be easy. What happened?

My math final was in the morning, but my mind refused to work. I had a baseball game in the afternoon and everyone was counting on me. My head was crammed so full of stuff it started to hurt. I wanted to phone Leah but didn't dare call her at this hour because her dad would probably freak out. I went to bed.

I lay there, in the dark, and tried to relax. Tried not to think. And then the headache hit, a sharp pain on both sides of my head, like pieces of steel pushing into my skull. My whole body felt tense, as if something terrible was about to happen.

Two hours went by and my headache got worse. I thought about those little pills. They fixed my shoulder. They should work on a headache. They were on the shelf, behind my baseball glove. Just one of them would help me relax and take all the pain away.

I switched on the light and slid out of bed. I swallowed one pill and put the bottle on the bedside table next to my water bottle. I fell asleep right after that, but woke up an hour later. My head still hurt and my nerves were shot. I needed sleep. I took another pill, put the bottle down and stared at it. Should I take one more? No. Two was enough. I tried to go back to sleep, but my mind was too busy pitching curveballs and solving equations. I worried about Leah too. I took another pill.

The next thing I knew, Mom was pounding on

my bedroom door. "Curt! Curt! Are you all right? It's time to get up!"

I felt so far away I couldn't answer. My tongue was heavy, too heavy to speak. My eyelids felt like they were glued shut. I was too dizzy to move.

"Curt?"

I forced myself to concentrate. "I'm fine, Mom." My feet crashed to the floor. I dragged my head up from the pillow. The room spun and my stomach lurched. I thought I was going to throw up.

I breathed deeply, sat very still and stared at the floor until the dizziness passed.

I don't want to think about that math test. It was like two hours of staring at a foreign language. I still felt sick, but forced myself to read the multiple-choice questions and check off my best guesses. I was thirsty and kept drinking from my water bottle. After a while I felt a little better, so I read the problems and worked out the ones that made any sense at all. But I didn't get anywhere near finished.

That was it. Done. Forget about it.

Like always, Stuart and I tossed the ball around before the game.

"Where's your girlfriend?" he asked. Leah always showed up early so we could talk.

"I don't know."

Coach put me in first. I stood on the pitcher's mound and glanced towards the stands. Where was Leah? The sun was too bright and dust clogged my throat. I started to feel dizzy again.

Okay. I had to focus on throwing that stupid little ball. I tried, but a headache started to nibble at the edges of my brain. My hand shook and my whole body trembled a little. The shaking was just enough to put me off, but not so much that anyone else would notice. Maybe I was sick. Could be the flu.

"Ball One."

Stay cool. You can handle this. I blinked, took a quick breath and focused on home plate. Wound up. Threw the ball. Fast. Perfect. Too low.

"Ball Two."

My nerves were getting to me. I took a deep breath. Tried to relax. Caught a glimpse of my dad standing behind the coach, arms folded across his belly. *Don't look at him.*

Can't help it. Dad shook his head and pulled

his eyebrows together. I knew that look. That look sucked all the confidence right out of me.

"Ball Three." I could not remember throwing it.

One more chance. I can do this. The batter grinned: so smug, so ready to walk. I glared at him. No way would I let him walk.

I stepped back, wound up, rolled forward, shifted my weight onto my left leg. The ball rocketed out of my hand. At the last second it curved. The batter jumped back, a narrow miss.

My father groaned.

We won that game — but only just, and no thanks to me. Coach pulled me after three innings. "Sorry," I told him, "I'm real tired. I was up all night studying." Slight exaggeration, but basically the truth. I put my hand over my eyes. "And I've got this killer headache." Whole truth.

"Curt," he said, "I know you like to tough it out and not take anything for pain, but trust me, if you took one of those pills I gave you, it would have helped you sleep last night."

If only it were that simple. Suddenly I was afraid all the pills would be gone and I couldn't get any more. "Well, Coach, you know me, I kind of — lost them."

"What?" he looked suspicious.

"Sorry, I don't know how it happened. But, listen, Coach, if you give me some more, I promise to be more careful." I was amazed at the way the lie slipped out of my mouth. And even more amazed that he believed me.

Coach reached into his pocket. "Go home," he said. "Get to bed early. And don't you dare get sick on me! We need you tomorrow." He put another little plastic bottle into my hand. "Rest that shoulder of yours, take it easy. You're uptight, Curt. Remember, one of those pills is plenty, and only when you really need it."

"Thanks, Coach." I walked away. No sign of my father. I figured he didn't want to stick around and be embarrassed by a loser son like me. I glanced at the stands one more time. No sign of Leah either.

I wouldn't make the same mistake again. I wouldn't take three pills in one night. I patted my glove and smiled. Now I had a good supply.

Chapter Five

When I came around the corner of the house, Dad was waiting with a baseball and glove. "You need to practice," he said.

I nodded. He was right.

He grinned and lightly punched my shoulder. "Come on, Curt."

Then I remembered the pill bottle, inside my glove, and knew he would never approve. "Dad, I need sleep. I'm going to lie down."

His smile vanished. "What? Don't you get

it, Curt? You're so goddamn lucky — you've got the build, you've got the talent, but you're going to waste it all because you're so bloody lazy!"

"Sure, Dad." I brushed past him into the house.

"Get back out here! Don't you dare walk away when I'm talking to you!"

I stopped. "Dad, I'm tired, okay? Coach Watson told me to get some sleep. I stayed up the last couple of nights studying."

"Why didn't you keep up with your work? If you study all term you don't need to cram the night before."

"I tried, I just — I don't get math! And I don't feel so good. I'm going to lie down."

I headed for the stairs. He thudded down the hall into his den and slammed the door so hard the walls shook.

"Hi, Mom." I walked into her office upstairs.

"Hi!" She leaned back from the computer. "How was the exam?"

"Brutal."

"Oh, that's too bad. Do you think you passed?"

"I don't know, Mom, it was hard. I just don't understand math."

"I know. I never liked it either, but if you're going to university…"

"Yeah, I need math. Even if I'll never use it again."

"What do you want to take?"

How many times had she asked me that lately? I almost told her then, almost said, *Nothing! I'm not going!*

"I don't know, Mom. I've got a headache, I'm gonna lie down."

Her brow wrinkled. "You get a lot of headaches these days. Maybe you should see the doctor."

"I'm fine, Mom, I'm just stressed out, with exams and all."

"I'll call you when dinner's ready."

"Sure, Mom, thanks."

I took a pill and lay down.

My head still hurt at dinner, but not so bad. If I sat really still I could hardly feel the pain. My stomach churned and I didn't think I'd be able to eat, but the chicken stir-fry Mom made was great. It slid down smoothly. My father didn't look up or speak, just ate, as if he was in a major hurry to get out the door.

"So, Curt," Mom said, trying to fill the silence, "are you ready for the game tomorrow?"

My father grunted. We ignored him. Sometimes I wonder how he manages at school. I mean, you'd think a teacher should be able to communicate better. How do his students figure out what the heck he's trying to say?

"Sure am. All I need is a good night's sleep. I'm looking forward to it — the game I mean, not the sleep." I ate some garlic toast. "Come to think of it, I'm looking forward to the sleep too. I'm real tired, Mom."

My father made a pained sound in his throat. He hates it when I rant on like that, which is the main reason I do it. That and because Mom and I can always catch a laugh. She likes to play with words and the sounds of them, like I do. Don't know why it bothers my dad so much, but I figure it's because he's no good at junk like that. Who knows?

I wish he'd lighten up.

Up in my room, I dialed Leah's number.

She answered on the first ring, her voice so low I could hardly hear.

"Leah? That you?"

"Curt! Yes! It's me…my dad's asleep."

"Where were you today?"

"Today?"

She sounded puzzled, as if she had forgotten all about it.

"Yes, today. The baseball game, *remember?* Seems to me you said something like, uh, now what was it? Oh yeah! *I wouldn't miss it!*"

"Oh! Curt! Listen, I'm so sorry but I couldn't make it because, well, it's because my, uh…"

She was obviously trying to think up a good excuse. I decided to help her out. "Because you had a headache, right?"

"Curt…"

"Well now, isn't that just too bad? Do you think you'll be well enough to show up tomorrow?"

"I don't know. And right now I don't much care!" She slammed the phone so hard it hurt my ear.

I lay on the bed with my biology book open on my chest. Why the heck did I take biology anyhow? Not that I hate it. I mean, it's not totally boring. The thing is, I had to take a science in grade eleven and my other choice was chemistry.

Dad teaches chemistry. If I messed up in chemistry I'd never hear the end of it. Even worse, he would probably want to help with my homework. So, I took biology.

I tried to study. The more I read, the more I realized that I'd never get through this book in one night. My head was already crammed so full of stuff, none of it made any sense. Another test. Another game. Another day.

My eyes shifted to the baseball glove sitting so innocently on top of my bookcase. Waiting. Holding a special promise in its fat, curled fingers. One pill would help me relax. I needed to relax. But I had taken too many the night before, and that morning I felt so sick it scared me.

I tried to focus on my textbook. Tried to stay awake, just for a couple more hours. My eyes closed, my book dropped. I picked it up. I stared at the small print. This was not working. So I went downstairs to make some coffee. I could stay awake until after midnight with a cup of strong coffee in me.

It worked. I studied until 1:00 and think I learned some. Then I crashed on the bed and fell asleep right away.

Chapter Six

I jerked awake. Glanced at the clock: 3:24. So late! So early! I lay there in the dark with my eyes squeezed shut, trying to sleep. Wide awake. If only my stupid brain would slow down.

I needed to be in good shape for the game. I loved baseball, I really did. Ever since I was a little kid, I practiced pitching by the hour. And I was good. I'm not bragging, simply stating a fact. I was good and I knew it. No question I was the best pitcher in our league. Except when I was tired. That's why I needed to fall asleep. Now. Had to. Couldn't.

Sometimes I got real scared.

What if I lost it? Couldn't pitch another ball? They were all counting on me. The team, Coach Watson, my father. Dad only loves the hero — he's ashamed of the screwup. I want him to be proud of me.

Okay. Push those thoughts away. Think about something nice, think about Leah. She forgot about the game. Did she meet someone else? Is she going to dump me?

It's not easy to relax simply because you want to.

Just one pill then. Just to help me sleep. Or not. I needed to cut back on them. Okay, but Coach gave me them to take when necessary, in an emergency.

Wasn't this an emergency? I glanced at those big red numbers again. 3:47. The big test. The big game. Tomorrow. I got out of bed and stumbled across the dark room to my bookcase. Picked up my baseball glove.

Mom let me sleep until 8:30. My exam was at 10:00. When I first woke up I felt so totally out of it I could barely walk straight. I was dizzy and felt like I was sleepwalking. Did I take more than one pill the night before? I couldn't remember.

I guess not, because once I showered and ate some breakfast, I felt okay.

The biology exam was grim, but I knew some of the answers. I might even have passed. Anyway, I was glad it was over. All I had left was English.

Then came the game. I got some good pitches in. Not my best, but good enough to win and put our team one step closer to the finals. Good enough so my father didn't walk away in disgust.

Leah didn't bother to show up.

When I got home I went straight to my room and called Leah. I heard the first ring before I remembered I was mad at her. Or she was mad at me. Whatever. The phone rang again.

I should hang up.

Too late. Someone picked up. Before I could speak there was a loud clunk in my ear. "Leah?"

Nothing.

Then a grunt, followed by heavy breathing and a fumbling sound, as if someone was having trouble holding onto the receiver. Finally a man's voice said, "Yeah?" Leah's dad.

I couldn't speak.

"Who is this?" he growled.

What could I say? Quietly I hung up the phone.

Stupid! Why did I do that?

What now? What an idiot! I stared at the phone. I couldn't call back now. I walked to the window and looked out. I remembered what I said before Leah hung up on me. Maybe it was kind of harsh, but she did miss the game and she didn't have a good reason.

I left my room, walked down the stairs and out of the house.

Traffic roared past as I walked along Esquimalt Road. I turned up Leah's street and stopped in front of her building. I stood there, looking up at the windows. What if she wasn't home? What if I buzzed and her father answered?

"What are you doing?"

I swung around. "Leah!"

She frowned at me over a bag of groceries. "Are you spying on me or something?"

"Spying? Of course not! I was trying to work up the nerve to push the buzzer."

"Since when are you afraid of buzzers?"

"It's not the buzzer I'm scared of, it's you!"

"Oh, fine then. I'll just go inside where you don't have to look at me." She stomped away.

"Wait, Leah! I came over to tell you I'm sorry for being rude on the phone."

She reached the door and stopped to look for her key.

"Leah, please. I phoned, but your dad answered and I hung up on him."

"Great!" she said. Still clutching the paper grocery bag, she tried to find her key in the pocket of her shorts.

"Leah, please. I acted like a jerk. I do that sometimes. I don't mean to, but it happens anyway. The thing is, I really like you and I miss you. Can't we start again?"

"No, we can't start again!" she shouted. She shoved the grocery bag at me.

I grabbed it and stood there like a big dope while she found her key and opened the door. She took the bag.

"Leah, at least walk down to Tim Hortons with me. I'll buy you a donut. We can talk."

"Sure."

"You mean it?"

"Of course. I said we couldn't start again. That doesn't mean we can't talk. Wait here. I'll be down in a minute."

We sat at a table, eating donuts and drinking pop. "I miss you at the games," I told her. "I messed up that first one when you didn't show."

"Sorry, I wanted to come, but my dad, he…" she paused, "…he just needed some help."

"Oh?"

She nodded, but changed the subject. "When's your next game?"

"Tomorrow at 5:00."

"I'll be there, cheering for you. I promise."

Chapter Seven

Stuart and I got to the field early. I was feeling pretty good; my shoulder didn't hurt at all. The night before I had taken one pill, just to be sure.

I threw a curveball to Stuart. He tried to catch it, missed and chased after it.

I wanted to turn around and see if Leah was there yet, but I had this weird feeling someone was standing behind me. I could almost picture my dad there, scowling, making me nervous. So I didn't look.

To my surprise, Stuart didn't throw the ball but walked up to me. "Did you see who's standing behind you?" he whispered.

"My dad?"

"Uh-uh," he grinned, "it's Rachel. You do realize she's got the hots for you, right?"

"Rachel? From work? Don't be such an idiot, Stuart, she's too old. Like you said, she likes to give us young guys a bad time."

"Whatever you say, man."

I turned and waved at her. "Hey, Rachel, are you going to watch our game?"

She grinned. "Sure am! I hear you're pretty good."

"You bet we are!"

Then I saw Leah coming up behind Rachel. "Leah!" I called and ran to meet her.

"How's it going, Curt?" She smiled, but the smile didn't light up her face the way it usually did.

"Good, I feel good. With you here, the other team doesn't stand a chance."

Her smile vanished. "Listen, Curt, whether you win or lose has nothing to do with me. You're the pitcher. I'm just here to enjoy the game."

"Right."

She laughed. "Don't look so bummed! I'm just saying that you're really good. If I miss a game, you can play just as well as ever."

"Whatever. So, do you want to go somewhere after? Go get something to eat?"

"Sure, Curt. Meanwhile, I'm cheering for you."

We won that game 8 to 1. I could do no wrong. Well, one wrong. If it hadn't been for that guy who made it to first base in the ninth inning, the score would have been 8 to 0. I almost had him too; the next two batters struck out. But the third one bunted past me. Our shortstop fumbled and the batter got to first. Meantime, the runner made it home.

After the game, Stuart came with us to get a burger, then Leah and I went for a walk to Macaulay Point. I showed her the round cement base where a huge cannon used to guard the strait during both world wars. "Stu and I used to play here when we were kids," I told her.

We leaned back on the warm cement, out of the wind. "I can hardly wait for school to start," she said.

"What? Are you nuts? Why?"

"I'm bored out of my mind! I couldn't find a job, I don't have any friends, and…"

"Aren't we friends?" I interrupted.

"Sure, Curt. But I mean girl friends. Besides, you're busy most of the time."

How was I supposed to answer that? "So, are you coming to the game on Saturday?"

"Wouldn't miss it."

That should have made me feel good. But it seemed to me she had said the same thing before.

Friday night I took a pill before I went to bed so I'd get a good sleep. I may have taken another one during the night, but I can't be sure. I may have dreamt it.

Saturday morning the rain was pouring down so hard I could barely see the neighbors' house. I thought the game would be canceled, so I phoned Leah to see if she wanted to catch a movie or something. No one answered.

The rain let up by noon. Stuart and I met at the field and took some practice pitches. I kept glancing around, hoping to see Leah.

"Sorry to disappoint you," Stuart grinned, "but Rachel won't be here today. She just started her shift when I was leaving. But she's on until late tonight, so you'll get to see her later."

I wound up and threw the ball at him. He

jumped out of the way. "Hey, watch it, man! You almost got me on the head."

I laughed. "If I'd been aiming for your head, you'd have some powerful headache right about now."

The game was about to start. Still no Leah.

I wasn't about to lose because of a girl. She was right. I played just fine before she came along and I could play just fine without her. All I had to do was concentrate. And ignore my father.

We won, but the score was 4 to 3, too close for comfort.

"You okay?" Coach Watson asked.

"Sure, why?"

"You seemed off your game today. Is something bothering you? Is your shoulder sore?"

"No, it's fine. We'll win the next game, no problem."

"I'm glad to hear that." He paused. "So, is it your girl?"

"What girl?"

He laughed. "That pretty girlfriend of yours. You think I haven't noticed how you play just great when she's here? But if she misses a game, you mess up."

"It has nothing to do with Leah."

"Okay. Whatever you say. But you take care of that arm and don't stay out all night before the next game!"

I waited, hoping he would offer me some more of those little pills, because I was almost out. But he started talking to someone else.

Stuart caught up with me on my way home to get changed for work. "Hey, man, you okay?"

"Why?"

"I don't know. You seem kind of stressed."

"No, I'm good."

"I was only kidding about Rachel, you know. You'd have to be out of your mind to look at her when you've got Leah."

"I know that."

But Leah didn't show up for the game.

Chapter Eight

After work I pushed out through the door. It wasn't dark yet, but gloomy, with a heavy rain beating down. I ducked my head and splashed across the wet parking lot.

I almost bumped into Rachel, standing there in a wet shirt that clung to her body. "Need a ride, Curt?" she asked.

Already my shirt was soaked through. "I'm fine. I don't have far to go."

"Where do you live?"

When I told her, she said, "That's on my way home. Get in, I'll drop you off. And don't worry," she grinned, "I promise not to seduce you on the way there."

"I didn't think…"

She laughed and opened the passenger door of a rusty little red car. "Get in." She walked around to the driver's side.

Rain streamed over my head as I stared at the open door. Rachel was being nice, offering me a ride. I got in.

"Where's your little girlfriend tonight?" she asked as she started the engine.

"She's busy."

"Stood you up, huh?"

"No."

"Did she come to your game?"

"No."

"Was she supposed to?"

I didn't answer.

"Poor Curt," she said. "Such a pretty little girl, but she doesn't appreciate you."

Still I didn't answer.

She took me home. To her place. "Come inside," she invited. "I'll make some coffee. You look cold."

I peered through the wet windshield. It was a grim scene. Paint was peeling from the walls of the run-down apartment building. A rusted-out truck was parked in front. "I really should be getting home. It's late."

"Listen," she said, "I don't know about you, but I'm hungry. As much as I'd like to go out for something to eat, I'm soaking wet. I need to get changed. So, I figure, why not have something here?"

"No thanks, I'll just walk home." I opened the car door.

She laughed. "I promise not to molest you. But I will make some coffee and grilled cheese sandwiches."

That sounded good. And, as usual, I was hungry. No harm in having something to eat. "Okay then, thanks."

Her apartment was in the basement. It was small and smelled of mold. I sat on a lumpy couch while she made coffee.

She opened the fridge. "I could go for a beer," she said. "Want one?" Before I could answer, she passed me a bottle and sat down next to me.

We drank the beer and talked about baseball. She seemed to know a lot about the game. "My old boyfriend used to play," she said.

I was really hungry by then. I wondered what had happened to those sandwiches she had mentioned. She got up and grabbed two more beers.

I stood up. "Uh, I really should get going."

She shoved a bottle at me. "Why? Is your girlfriend waiting?" She winked. "Besides, I'm gonna make those sandwiches now." She sipped her beer and wandered into the tiny kitchen. She put on a CD and danced as she opened a loaf of bread that lay on the counter.

I drank my beer and waited. I was so hungry that the beer was going straight to my head. Finally she put some sandwiches on the coffee table and went back to open the fridge. "Oops!" she laughed. "I'm out of beer."

"Coffee would be good," I told her.

"Whatever you say." She laughed even harder as she poured coffee into two mugs. When she came back to the couch she had something in her hand — a little square of cardboard that was folded up like an envelope. She opened it and sprinkled something onto a hand mirror. A pure white powder. She divided it in half, stuck a short straw up one nostril and snorted the powder.

"Cocaine?" I asked.

"Yeah," she said, "it's way better than beer. Try some." She pushed it towards me. "Go on, it won't hurt you."

I should have said no. But I just stared at that innocent-looking white powder and said nothing.

She laughed at me. "What's the matter? Scared? Will your mommy and daddy ground you? Will your little girlfriend get mad?"

Whether it was the beer on an empty stomach or the way she made me feel like a little kid, I don't know. But I tried it. Wow! I had never known anything like it. The high was so sudden I was bursting out of my skin. I felt so good it hurt!

Then, just as suddenly, it was over. I felt real bad. So bad I could not stay in her smelly little apartment one second longer. I felt myself sinking lower and lower. My skin itched. I felt filthy.

Rachel's laugh followed me as I hurried out the door into the rain. "You'll be back!" she called.

Her words rang in my ears. I never wanted to see her again.

When I opened our back door and stepped into the kitchen, I noticed a light in the living room. The door squeaked as I eased it closed.

"Is that you, Curt?" Mom called.

"Where have you been?" Dad yelled.

"Oh, Curt!" My mother ran into the kitchen and threw her arms around me. "We were so worried! We almost called the police!"

"Why?"

Dad came in and snapped the light on. "Do you have any idea what time it is? We expected you home after work! Where were you?"

"It's not that late."

"Curt," Mom said, "we've been sitting here for hours. Why didn't you phone? You always tell us if you're going to be late!"

"Sorry, I went to see Leah after work."

"Don't lie to us!" my father shouted.

"Curt," Mom told me, "I phoned Leah hours ago. She said she hadn't seen you. She said to tell you she's sorry she missed the game, but her father is sick."

Her dad was sick? Was that why she missed the game? I looked from Mom to Dad. Water trickled down my forehead and dripped off my shirt onto the floor. I couldn't think of anything to say.

"And don't tell us you were at Stuart's," Dad warned. "Your mom phoned him too."

"I just…this girl from work gave me a ride. We had something to eat and we were just talking. I guess I lost track of time. I'm sorry."

"You should be," Dad said. He sniffed. "Have you been drinking?"

I nodded. "A beer."

"Please, Curt, just phone us next time?" Mom asked.

"Sure, I promise. But I'm real tired now. I'm going to bed."

"You shouldn't be drinking!" my father called after me. "You're underage!"

Chapter Nine

The next day was Sunday. I didn't need to work until 11:00. Good thing too, because it was all I could do to drag myself out of bed at 10:00.

Mom was sitting at the kitchen table, drinking coffee and staring out the window. She looked awful. Her eyes were red and her face was all puffy.

"Hi, Mom!" I smiled and tried to look cheerful, even if I felt terrible.

"Morning, Curt." She looked at me like I was

a stranger. She didn't smile. "There's coffee if you want some. And cereal." She studied the empty bowl in front of her, then pushed it towards me. "I don't feel like eating right now."

"Are you sick?"

She shook her head. "No. I'm just…I had a bad night." When I didn't answer, she went on. "I'm worried about you, Curt."

I shrugged and poured myself some coffee. I filled the bowl with cereal.

"Do you have a new girlfriend?" she asked.

"No, Mom. It's nothing like that." Somehow I couldn't bring myself to use Rachel's name. "We just went out for something to eat. And we talked about baseball. Her boyfriend plays baseball too."

"Oh. So she has a boyfriend?"

"Yes, she's way old."

I munched on my cereal. Mom sipped her coffee. "Why did you lie?"

"What?"

"Last night, why did you tell us you were with Leah?"

"Oh that! I don't know, Mom. I thought Leah would be jealous if she found out. I figured if no one else knew, she'd never find out." My mom's questions were driving me nuts. I had to get away from there.

"Do you really think that's fair to Leah?" she asked.

"I don't know…whatever." I scooped up the last of my cereal, took a swig of coffee and stood up. "I've got to go or I'll be late for work."

"Hey, Stuart," I said when I arrived at the store, "I thought you had today off."

"I'm supposed to, but Rachel didn't show — again. And they needed someone on cash. So, they called me at the last minute."

I was glad Rachel wouldn't be in today.

"Where were you last night?" Stuart asked. "Your parents sounded worried."

I could not tell him I was with Rachel. I needed a quick, believable lie. "I ran into some friends after work and we went out for something to eat. No big deal. I wasn't that late, but you know how parents are."

"What friends?"

Nothing like being put on the spot. I tried to think of someone I knew that Stuart didn't. Baseball buddies, friends from school, people at work, he knew them all. "What is this?" I snapped. "Twenty Questions? I've got one mom, thanks. I don't need another one!"

I turned away from the hurt look on Stuart's face. I didn't need this. Who did he think he was? I felt pretty bad though. Later on, when I saw him head off for his break alone, I felt even worse.

I phoned Leah as soon as I got home. There was no answer. I left a message, but she didn't call back. Later, I tried two more times, but Leah never returned my calls.

That night I was almost asleep when it suddenly hit me that Leah was mad at me again. What did I do this time? Maybe she had found out about Rachel. For sure she knew I was out late, because my mother told her.

I lay there half-asleep, worrying about Leah and the next day's baseball game, first of the semi-finals against the Panthers. I knew the Panthers were a strong team, with a couple of awesome hitters. My head started to hurt. Next thing I knew, I was thinking about Rachel. Not Rachel so much as what she gave me. I kept thinking about that cocaine and how good it made me feel. But the low afterward was hard to shake.

I couldn't sleep. I had to stop thinking. I got up and took two pills. Only two left.

On my way to the game Monday evening I stopped by Leah's place, but no one was home. I arrived at the field angry enough to spit.

"Hey, Curt!" Stuart called. He seemed to have forgotten the way I had talked to him. We tossed the ball back and forth as usual. But I didn't feel that great and I couldn't seem to concentrate.

My fastball needed work. I wound up and threw the ball. Stuart ducked just in time.

"Are you trying to kill me?"

"Sorry, man! I was thinking about Leah!"

"Leah? I thought you liked her!"

"So did I!" said a surprised voice behind me. I swung around. "Leah!"

Her eyes were huge and she looked scared.

I dropped my glove and ran around the fence. "Leah! Where have you been?"

"Nowhere. I've just been, uh, busy. Curt, what did you mean you were thinking about me when you tried to hit Stuart with the ball?"

"What? I didn't try to hit him! I just — I wasn't concentrating."

"Good thing he ducked!"

"Yeah." I ached to put my arms around her, but I wasn't sure if she would let me. "Let's walk for a minute."

We started around the field. "Your mom phoned Saturday night," Leah said. "She was worried about you."

"Yeah, well, I went out with some friends after work. I was kind of late and should have phoned, but I forgot."

"My dad would kill me if I did that!"

"That would solve the problem all right!"

She laughed.

"How is your dad?"

She frowned. "What do you mean?"

"Mom told me he was sick."

"Oh that!" She looked away. "He hasn't been feeling so good since we moved here."

Chapter Ten

The score was Falcons 6, Panthers 0. I felt like a superstar. The bottom of the eighth was about to begin and the first Panther walked up to bat. While he took some practice swings I glanced at the stands, just to see Leah, for good luck. What I saw sent a chill through my bones. Rachel was making her way across the grass towards the stands. I pulled my eyes away.

Okay, I could do this. I could get this guy out. All I had to do was concentrate. He wasn't a great hitter. He shouldered the bat. My eyes flicked over to the stands just as Rachel sat down in front of Leah. She smiled at me and waved.

My guts twisted. I turned away. Everyone was quiet. Watching, waiting. I took a quick breath, wound up and pitched. The batter swung and connected. On second base, Jarrod caught the fly ball. I lucked out.

My eyes kept sneaking over to the stands. Rachel and Leah were watching me. Not talking. Of course not, what did I think? I mean, it wasn't like they knew each other. But it gave me the creeps, the two of them sitting so close.

By the end of the inning the score was 6-2.

We scored one run in the ninth and then I was back in the spotlight. Or on the spot. But with the score at 7-2, we couldn't lose. Could we?

I tried to avoid looking at the stands, but my eyes were drawn there anyway. Rachel was twisted around, talking to Leah.

The next Panther made it to second. Leah was gone.

They scored four runs in that last inning. So, final score 7-6. We won, but I had screwed up. I felt bad. I didn't wait for the coach to ask about my shoulder, or for the team to give me a bad time. I took off for Leah's place.

She was standing near the spruce tree in front of her building when I got there. "Leah!" I caught up, puffing, out of breath. "I thought we were going out after the game."

"How could you?" She kept her back to me, fists clenched at her sides.

"How could I what?" I placed my hands on her shoulders and gently turned her around. Tears streamed down her face.

"How could you go out with that *Rachel* person?"

"I didn't go out with her; she just gave me a ride home after work. It was raining…"

"Don't lie to me, Curt! I know how late you were Saturday night. Your mother phoned me, remember? And Rachel told me everything!"

"But…there's nothing to tell!"

"She told me about the drugs, Curt. And, you know? I can't handle it. I've got enough problems without you doing drugs!"

"Once! I just tried it once! It won't happen again."

She shook her head. "Maybe not, Curt. I hope

not, for your sake." She sighed. "I'm tired. I'm going inside now."

"So, when will I see you?"

She looked up at me and for a minute I thought everything was going to be all right. "I don't know, Curt."

"But, Leah, you can't do this! Just because I tried coke? Once?"

"It's not only that. It's everything! I can't trust you, Curt. You're not the guy I thought you were."

She turned and walked towards the door. I ran after her. "You're wrong, you know. Sure I've had a few problems lately, but I'm fine now. Please, Leah, give me another chance!"

She stood on her toes and kissed me on the cheek, like she might kiss her brother. "Stay clean," she whispered, "and we'll see what happens."

I watched helplessly as the door closed quietly behind her.

I walked until I reached the waterfront. A fresh, cool wind blew against my face. I could see clear across the strait to the Olympic Mountains of Washington state.

Leah liked the waterfront too; she said it

made her feel free. I stared down at the waves. I had to get her back.

I sat on the edge of the old gun emplacement. A headache was starting behind my eyes and I tried to remember if I had any more pills at home. It seemed like I needed more and more of them lately.

I made a promise to myself: I would stop taking those pills forever.

As soon as baseball season was over.

A block away from home I saw the rusty red car. The door opened and Rachel stepped out.

"Hiya, Curt. Where's your girlfriend?"

"None of your business!"

"Ah, now, Curt, that's no way to talk to Rachel." She slunk over and placed her hand on my chest. "What's the matter, did little Leah dump you?" She slipped something into my pocket.

"Stay out of my life!"

Rachel laughed. "Catch you next time!" She got into her car and drove away.

I reached into my pocket and pulled out a little piece of cardboard, folded up like an envelope. I stuffed it deep inside my baseball glove.

Chapter Eleven

From the kitchen I heard Mom and her friends talking in the living room. I made myself a sandwich, grabbed a glass of milk and carried them upstairs. I threw my glove on the floor and kicked it under my desk.

When I finished eating I stared at the phone. I wanted to call Leah so badly! I could see her face, her bright smile, I could hear her laugh and feel her soft skin. But I couldn't phone, not now. My head hurt, my stomach churned. I picked up the pill bottle. Two left. I needed to save them.

I flopped backward on my bed and tried to relax. But now all I could think of was my baseball glove, under the desk. I couldn't leave it there. Finally I got up, retrieved the glove, pulled out that little package, opened one small flap, then another. I stared at the soft white powder. Why did Rachel give it to me? I should flush it down the toilet.

Mom was busy with her friends. Dad was away overnight on a fishing trip. Who would know? I remembered how good it made me feel. And right now I felt so bad! Just one more time then. What harm could it do? I picked up a sheet of paper, ripped it to a smaller size and rolled it into a tube.

The high was even better than I remembered. Nothing mattered. Not a stupid little baseball game. Not Leah. Nothing. If only I could feel this way forever. If only the high would last a lifetime!

But it didn't. When I crashed I felt worse than before. Sick. But hungry. I went downstairs, made another huge sandwich, poured myself a coffee from the carafe and went back up to my room. After eating every crumb I lay on the bed and tried to think. One thing for sure, I had to stop taking those stupid little pills from Coach Watson. Then my problems would be over. It's not like I needed them or anything.

I would stay away from cocaine. That stuff was bad news. I mean, it grabs a hold of you somehow. It lurks in your brain like the notes of a song that won't leave you alone. Never again. If I didn't watch it I would end up in a moldy apartment and drive a rusty old car.

I pushed Rachel from my mind and thought about Leah instead. A little self-control and I would be back to normal, feeling good. We could get back together. No problem.

If only I didn't have to play baseball. The whole team depended on me. I glanced at the numbers on my clock. 1:17. Tomorrow's game was in the morning. I needed sleep. But I was wide awake. I rotated my right arm. A stab of pain shot through my shoulder. My nerves were on edge. Pain played at the corners of my mind.

That little bottle waited on my bedside table. There were only two pills left. I flipped my pillow over and sank into its coolness. I thought about tomorrow morning. We had to win.

I checked my clock again. How did it get to

be 2:04? If I lay awake all night, I would be a mess in the morning and we would lose for sure. I mean, our other pitcher, to put it kindly, sucks.

I switched on the light, reached over and shook a pill out of the bottle. Just one, because I didn't think I should mix the pills with the cocaine in my body. I placed the last pill and my water bottle beside the clock and sank into my pillow.

"Go away!" I tried to yell. But my voice was no more than a moan. Who was banging on my door in the middle of the night? I had finally fallen asleep and now someone was waking me up! My arms and legs were heavy and wooden; my eyes refused to open.

The banging got louder. "Curt!" my mother yelled. "It's after 9:00!"

"Go away!" I yelled.

"Doesn't your game start at 10:00?"

I threw the covers from my face. The room was bright with sunshine. I looked at the clock and couldn't believe my eyes. It was 9:05.

"Curt? Are you all right? Are you up yet?"

I dropped my feet to the floor. "Yes."

"I made you some breakfast."

I sat up. My head felt fuzzy and my stomach heaved. "I'm not hungry. I'm going to have a quick shower."

"Okay then, you can take a bagel with you. I'll drive you to the game."

"Thanks, Mom."

When she dropped me off she said, "Curt, I wish I could stay but I have an appointment in town. I'll try to get back before the game is over."

"No problem."

"Hey, Curt, what happened to you?" Stuart asked.

I figured what he meant was, *Why didn't you get here in time to do some warm-up pitches?*

"I slept in. No big deal."

"I didn't mean that," Stuart said. "I meant, what happened to your face? You look awful." He stepped closer. "Is it because of Leah? I saw her at the store and she told me she was going away for a while. Sorry, man."

"Can't you just leave me alone?"

Stuart stared. Then he turned and walked to first base. I stepped up to the pitcher's mound, feeling like I was in a plastic bag. I could see everything around me just fine, but I didn't feel like I was part of it. Sounds came from far away and my arms and legs felt heavy, like when you first wake up from a really deep sleep.

I kept thinking about Leah. Where did she go? Why didn't she tell me?

"I'm taking you out, Curt," Coach Watson told me after the third inning. We were losing five runs to three.

"What? You can't do that!"

"Oh? That's strange, I thought I was coach of this team." He placed a hand on my shoulder. I shrugged it off. "Curt, you're not playing well right now. Take a rest, go toss some practice balls. Maybe I'll put you back in later."

"Forget it!" I shouted and threw down my glove. I knew I was acting like a jerk, but I couldn't stop myself. I couldn't control the rage that flared inside me.

"Curt, what's wrong with you? Are you sick or something?"

"Yes, I'm sick! I'm sick of baseball! I'm sick of you! I'm…" I paused when I saw the shock on Coach's face, but somehow that made me angrier. "I quit!"

I stomped off the field.

Chapter Twelve

"Curt!" Coach yelled. "You can't walk out on me in the middle of a game!"

I ignored him and kept walking, fists clenched at my sides, shoulders tense. Someone grabbed my sleeve. I yanked my arm away. "Hey, Curt, what's going on?"

I swung around. Stuart's face was white and his eyes bugged out. He stared at me like I'd lost my mind. The rage boiled over. "Have you got a problem?"

"No," he said. "Have you?"

"Yes!" I yelled into his face. "And guess what. It's you!"

His head jerked back as if I had slugged him. "I'm going back to the game," he said quietly.

Even before I reached the sidewalk I was sorry. I stopped and turned around. No one looked at me. The game started up without me. So I walked away. I had no idea where I was going. I just kept walking and walking, trying not to think.

Hours later, when I got home, Mom met me at the door. "Curt! I've been so worried. What happened?"

"What do you mean?"

"I went to the game and your coach told me you quit! I can't believe it. You love baseball!"

"I used to love baseball," I corrected. "Things change."

"But Curt, I don't understand. How can you quit now? Even if you're tired of the game, it isn't fair to your team."

"They can go screw themselves for all I care!" I yelled.

"Curt!" Mom was so shocked, tears spurted out of her eyes. I've never seen anything like it.

I mean, she hadn't been crying until then, but there they were, big wet tears shooting down her face.

I felt bad. "Mom! I'm sorry!" I gave her a hug.

"It wasn't my fault," I told her a few minutes later, while we made ourselves some lunch. "I threw a few bad pitches and Coach Watson took me off."

"That doesn't seem fair. He knows you're the star player."

"Yeah, well that's why I quit."

"You lost your temper, Curt, but you can still go back. You can call your coach and talk to him."

"No way. I'm through with baseball!"

When I arrived for work at 4:00, the first person I saw was Rachel. I tried to ignore her, but there she was, behind the cash register. She winked. I hurried for the stockroom. Stuart was stacking boxes on a trolley and he acted like I didn't exist.

I tried to think of something to say. Like, *Hey, man, sorry I walked out on the game and all.* But nothing came out. He walked away, wheeling the trolley. I had to say something. "Did we win?"

"What do you think?" He pushed through the doors.

Then the manager walked in. "So, Curt," he

said, "I see you finally decided to show up."

"What? It's just 4:00!"

"Right. I asked you to start at 3:00."

After work I stepped out to a warm summer evening, with the sun still bright in the sky. Stuart was standing on the sidewalk, his back to me. He had ignored me all shift, just like I had ignored Rachel. This was my chance then; I would walk up to him and tell him I was sorry for being such a jerk.

Before I could move, a car pulled up in front of Stuart with three guys from our team in it. If they had yelled at me I could have handled it, but they didn't. They didn't even bother to look at me. Stuart climbed into the backseat and the car took off.

Cool fingers slipped around my arm. "What happened to your friends?" Rachel asked.

"I messed up."

"And they took off on you? That bites."

I shrugged and started to walk away, even though I dreaded going home because my father would be back by now. That's when I realized Rachel was still clinging to my arm. "Let's get something to eat," she said.

My first thought was to say no. But, hey, who else wanted anything to do with me? "Let's not go to your place."

She shook her head. "I promise."

I thought we would go to a coffee shop, but we ended up at a little square house with peeling paint and a yard full of junk. Music belched from the doors and windows. "My friends are having a party," she explained. "There'll be lots of food."

She was right. There was lots of food and drugs and booze. Soon after we got there I found a phone and called home. Luckily my mother answered. "I'm at a party with my friends," I told her, "so don't worry if I'm late."

I have no idea what time Rachel drove me home. I only remember when I woke up the next morning I wished I was dead, I felt so bad. My head ached. The light hurt my eyes. I covered my face with my pillow. I might never get out of bed. Then my bedroom door crashed open.

"Curt?"

It was my father. I groaned.

"What's wrong? Are you sick?"

"No."

"Your mom said you quit the Falcons!"

When I didn't answer he yanked the pillow from my face.

"Have you lost your mind?"

"I'm sick of baseball!"

He sank onto the chair by my desk. "It's all because of that girl! She wants you to quit, right? She wants you to spend all your time with her!"

"It has nothing to do with Leah."

"You've got to call Coach Watson and apologize."

"Apologize? For what? He's the one who took me out of the game."

My father hopped to his feet, his face bright red. "Listen. Either you apologize, or..." He stopped, like he couldn't think of anything to say.

"Or what?"

"Or you'll be sorry."

"Sure, Dad. Maybe I'm sorry I ever started playing baseball."

His jaw dropped. I could see the hurt in his eyes and tried not to care. The words in my head were, *Look, Dad, I'm sorry. I just need some time off, okay? Time to sort things out.* Those words were so clear I almost thought I had said them out loud.

He turned and walked away. Just like everyone else in my life.

Chapter Thirteen

I thought about Leah every day. I watched for her in the store, but she never came by. I phoned, but no one answered. Then one day, as I was leaving for my lunch break, I saw this tall, good-looking dude in the parking lot.

"Hey!" I called. "Hey, Darren!"

He frowned. "Do I know you?"

"Yes. Well, no, not exactly. I'm Curt. I know your sister."

His face tightened. "Yeah?"

"Is she okay? I haven't seen her for a while!"

He studied my face, as if trying to decide whether to answer.

"Listen," I said, "I only want to know if she's okay. Have you got a minute for coffee? I'll buy."

Darren's eyes narrowed, then he nodded.

He sat across from me in a booth.

"So? Did something happen to her?"

"Leah's fine now. She's staying at my place for a while. She had a rough time with Dad."

"Is your dad still sick?"

He gave me a strange look. "Didn't Leah tell you? Dad's an alcoholic. He's been way worse since Mom left. He lost his job, the house, everything, but he still kept denying he had a problem. After they moved here, Dad got so bad, Leah was scared to stay with him anymore so she moved into my place."

"Is he okay?" I asked. "I mean, no one ever answers the phone."

"That's because, after Leah took off, he got scared. He finally admitted he needed help. He's in detox now."

"Oh. That's good then."

Darren nodded. "It was either that or drink himself to death."

No wonder Leah was so upset. "Listen, Darren, do you think she would talk to me if I phoned?"

"Don't ask me. She never talks about what happened between you two. One thing I can tell you though, if you ever lie to my sister, if you show any hint of a problem with drugs or alcohol, that girl will drop you like a hunk of lead."

"Right," I said. "No problem."

I was back at work before I realized that I didn't get the phone number.

I had no idea there were so many Johnsons in the phone book. I started with the ones in Esquimalt and called every D. Johnson until I hit pay dirt. "Hi, this is Darren's place. Please leave your name …" I hung up, wrote the number on a sheet of paper, folded it and slid it into my pocket.

I missed baseball, but no one else seemed to care, no one asked me to come back. Stuart totally ignored me. My father acted like I didn't exist. I guess that's why I started hanging out more and more with Rachel and her friends. Party time. There were always loads of people around and plenty of drugs and booze. "Hey, Curt," Rachel shouted over the music and voices one night. "Want to try something different? It's cheap and it works real fast. You'll love it!"

That's when I first smoked crack. Rachel was right. The high hits so fast you don't see it coming. And, if you're lucky, it lasts for all of five minutes before you start to crash. That low is so low you need to keep using and using, spending more and more money.

But I was okay. I only used at parties. I could handle it.

Sometimes, when I was alone in my room at night, I got to thinking about how I had messed up. And then I felt so bad I couldn't sleep. I needed help, but Coach's pills were long gone. So I started keeping a stash of crack with me, just in case. Kind of like those pills, for emergencies only. I could handle it. No problem.

One day when no one else was home, I slept late, then went to the kitchen and made myself a sandwich. There was some coffee in the carafe so I poured myself a mug and sat at the table. The back door opened and Mom walked in. She poured herself some coffee and sat across from me.

She looked at me and then stared into her coffee mug. She lifted it and put it down again. "Curt, something's wrong. Please tell me, maybe I can help."

"I'm fine!"

"You've dropped your old friends, you've quit sports, we hardly ever see you — and you seem so unhappy…"

"So I made some new friends! Is that a crime?"

"Of course not, Curt, it's just that you've changed so much lately." She took a deep breath and went on. "I've done some research. Curt, you have all the symptoms of having a drug addiction."

I felt that rage again. It built inside me so fast I couldn't control it. "You're out of your mind!"

"Curt, you need help…"

"Stay out of my life!" I yelled.

I heard her sob as I slammed out of the house. I felt so bad I wanted to go back, but my feet kept right on walking until I found myself at Rachel's place.

She was sitting on her lumpy couch, smoking a joint, drinking beer and crying. Black mascara

streaked down her face. The roots of her hair were
black too.

"What happened to you?"

"I got fired! I can't believe it! I always work
hard, I do a good job — but that manager never
liked me."

She was right. She did do a good job when
she was there, but half the time she showed up
late or not at all.

"I'm going to need that money you owe me,"
she said.

"What money?"

She laughed. "Come on, kid, you didn't think
all that stuff was free, did you?"

"But I paid you!" I couldn't believe this.
Almost all of my last paycheck went to Rachel.
She said it was my share of the party expenses.

Her laughter died and her face turned hard.
"No. I've been keeping track. You still owe me
plenty. And I owe plenty to a couple other guys,
so I need you to pay up."

"Whatever. I have no money until payday."

"Sorry, kid. No way I can wait that long. I
need the money now. Trust me, you don't want
to mess with these guys."

Rachel didn't look so good; she was pale like a

ghost. When she smiled, a shudder ran through me because her face looked exactly like a skull. She raised her hand to take a drag and it shook so bad she could hardly reach her mouth.

Had she just threatened me? Or was she scared? I didn't stick around to find out.

Chapter Fourteen

I walked straight to Leah's apartment building and stared up at the windows. They stared back like dark, empty eyes. Leah wasn't there.

I hated myself. I hated what I was doing to my life. I hated this *thing*, this terrible need. It was inside me, around me, creeping over my skin. I had to make it stop. But I couldn't! I was so weak! I hated myself.

Suddenly the anger took over. Everything was Leah's fault. If she hadn't dumped me I

Dayle Campbell Gaetz

would be fine. Trembling, I ran to the door and pounded on the buzzer, over and over again.

"Hey!" a woman yelled from the window next to Leah's. "Give it up! What are you, crazy?"

I stepped back and shook my fist up at her, an old lady with gray hair. "Mind your own business!" I screamed and took off down the street.

I walked for hours without going anywhere. By evening my feet hurt. I was hungry and headed for home. I was almost at the backyard when I heard voices. I crept slowly to the corner of the house. Mom and Dad were on the back porch, talking.

My father said, "He lost his job?"

"Yes. The manager phoned. He said Curt didn't show up for work today and this isn't the first time. He has to let him go."

My face went hot. Anger burned in my gut. What was she talking about? I never missed work! Not on purpose anyway. Sometimes the manager changed the schedule on me, but it wasn't my fault. No one told me I was supposed to work today!

"Where is he now?" my father asked.

I could barely hear my mother's answer. "I

don't know." She paused. "Doug, I'm scared."

I crept away and headed for the store. I would tell that manager exactly what I thought of him. He said to come in on Tuesday, not today.

I stormed across the parking lot, angry enough to throttle the guy. "Ten Percent Off Everything in the Store!" the big sign across the front windows said. How stupid can you get? Someone put it up too early. That's supposed to be for tomorrow. The parking lot was full, just like on Tuesdays. And suddenly it hit me. I had messed up, again. Today was Tuesday. I turned away.

I was hungry and really wanted to go home, but could not face up to my parents, not right then. So I kept on walking. My feet hurt more with every step and my head was starting to feel worse than my feet. When I saw the pay phone I stopped and stared at it. Should I call her? Would she hang up on me? Did I still have the number? I searched my pockets and found a folded sheet of paper.

I didn't have any money, but I made the call anyway. I needed to talk to her so badly I called collect. Instead of giving my name, I quickly said, "Leah, please talk to me!"

She answered. I held my breath. The mechanical voice said, "You have a collect call from 'Leah, please talk to me!' Will you accept the charges?" She gasped. I waited.

"Yes!"

"Leah," was all I could say.

"Curt, where are you?"

"I'm ... walking."

"I feel like walking," she said. "Where are you?"

Something was wrong here, but my head hurt, I couldn't think. "I gotta go now." I hung up, stared at the phone and walked away.

At the gun emplacement I hunched down out of the cold wind. I was safe here and might never go home. If only I wasn't so cold and hungry. If only my head didn't hurt so bad. And I was tired. I would rest a while and then decide what to do.

"Curt!" The voice seemed far away. "Curt!"

My eyes refused to open. My voice wouldn't work. I was in the middle of a deep dream. But I was so cold. All of my bones ached. I must have been asleep for a very long time. I realized that someone was leaning over me. A warm hand rested on my arm. "Curt? Are you okay?"

"Mmm…"

Hands gripped my shoulders, shook me. "Curt, talk to me!"

"Leah?" My eyes opened. Everything was dark. I could see only vague outlines against a slate gray sky.

"You've been missing for hours. I — we were hoping we'd find you here."

My head throbbed. I pressed my hands against it.

"It's all right now, Curt, it's time to go home."

"No…don't understand…can't go home… Mom and Dad…"

"Your parents are worried sick about you. So is Stuart. Everyone has been looking for you all night!"

"Stu?"

"I'm here, man."

"How'd you guys find me?"

"Your mom phoned," Stuart said, "and said you took off. Just lucky I knew where Leah was staying. I called her just before you did. Then we went out looking. It took us a while, but we finally figured out you might be here."

"We want to help you, Curt," Leah said.

Suddenly I was on guard. I sat up straight.

"What is this? What's going on?"

"Nothing, man," Stuart said. "It's just, we're real worried, you know, about the problems you're having."

"Yeah? What *problems?*"

"Okay, since you asked, your problems with drugs."

"I'm out of here." But before I could move, Leah grabbed my hand and held it tight. "Please, Curt, come back to your house with us. We need to talk to your parents."

"Yeah?"

"Yes," Stuart said. "You have some better place to go?"

He had me there. "I don't have a problem with drugs."

"My dad talked the same way," Leah said. "He couldn't see what alcohol was doing to him. Not even when my mom left him and he lost his job and our house."

"So? That's got nothing to do with me."

"Curt," she said, "don't you get tired of pretending to be all right when, inside, you're hurting so bad it terrifies you?"

How does she know? "There is no problem."

"You know, I learned a lot about addiction

because of my dad. It's a disease, Curt, and if you don't already have it, then you're so close you can't see straight. We need to go home and talk to your mom and dad. They can help. Trust me."

"Don't worry, we'll both stick with you," Stuart said. "The thing is, we all know about it now, me, Leah, your mom and dad. So you don't need to pretend anymore. Doesn't that take the load off, old buddy?"

Strange, but it did feel good. If everyone knew, then there was nothing to hide, nothing to lie about. Before I could answer, Leah and Stuart helped me to my feet. My legs ached from being cramped up in the cold. My head throbbed.

A bright orange sunrise colored the sky as my friends walked, one on each side of me, towards home.

orca soundings

Orca Soundings is a teen fiction series that features realistic teenage characters in stories that focus on contemporary situations and problems.

Soundings are short, thematic novels ideal for class or independent reading. Written by such stalwart authors as William Bell, Beth Goobie, Sheree Fitch and Kristin Butcher, there will be between eight and ten new titles a year.

For more information and reading copies, please call Orca Book Publishers at 1-800-210-5277.

Other titles in the Orca Soundings series:

DAYLE CAMPBELL GAETZ is the
bestselling author of more than half a dozen
books for young readers. Her book *Mystery
from History* was short-listed for a Silver Birch
Award. Dayle is a full-time author and creative
writing instructor. She lives in Campbell River,
BC.

DATE DUE			